Three Little Lambs... Somewhere

Written by Susan Amundson

Illustrated by Brenda Geiken

ISBN 1-59984-002-2

Published by bluedoor, LLC
     6595 Edenvale Boulevard, Suite 155
     Eden Prairie, MN 55346
     800-979-1624
     www.bluedoorpublishing.com

Printed in the United States of America.
10 9 8 7 6 5 4 3 2 1

To Our Children and Their Loving Pets.

2006

Susan Olmundson

Three little lambs
All plush and white

Are bathed and brushed
With such delight

Feeding and brushing
Are part of the plan

Then off to the fair
Will go all three lambs

Now three little girls
Want bikes in their hands

But to have these bikes
They must sell their lambs

"We know bikes are fun.
We love our dear lambs.

Their question is asked
Of Daddy, so kind

He scratches his head
The answer he finds

The bikes can be earned
By doing some chores

They keep their dear lambs
To love and adore

But three little lambs
No longer feel loved

The girls want new bikes
Instead of their hugs

Next day all three girls
Return from the town

And see that their lambs
Are nowhere around

They hunt and they hunt
But nothing is found

Not even lamb's wool
Or a baaa kind of sound

Three bikes are being earned
As girls work for pay

They mow the big lawn
And push carts of hay

But...bikes aren't the same
As love from their lambs

Three smart little girls
Think up a new plan

"Oh! Daddy," they say
"We want our lambs back.

Return all three bikes
For cash in a sack."

So tired from working
They listen to Dad,
"Money can't buy
The love that you had.

You've earned those new bikes,
They are yours to keep
But maybe your lambs
Will come while you sleep."

Three lambs must have heard
How much they were missed

Three bikes just don't give
A hug and a kiss

"Oh! Daddy was right,
How smart he must be!

He knows lambs and bikes
Are different, we see."

Now later that day
Returning from town

Three soft, happy lambs
Are smiling when found

Their eyes meet the girls
With baaas full of love

And arms wrap their wool
With joy and a hug

Three Little Lambs were...

Somewhere!